THE CLUE IN THE CRYSTAL BALL

Look for these books in the
Clue™ series:

Clue™

THE CLUE IN THE CRYSTAL BALL

Book created by A. E. Parker

Written by Dona Smith

Based on characters from the Parker Brothers game

A Creative Media Applications Production

SCHOLASTIC INC.
New York Toronto London Auckland Sydney

For Karen

Special thanks to: Susan Nash, Laura Millhollin, Maureen Taxter, Jean Feiwel, Ellie Berger, Craig Walker, Greg Holch, Kim Williams, Nancy Smith, Veronica Ambrose, David Tommasino, Jennifer Presant, and Elizabeth Parisi.

ISBN 0-590-13744-1

12 11 10 9 8 7 6 5 4 3 2 1   7 8 9/9 0 1 2/0

Printed in the U.S.A.   40

First Scholastic printing, July 1997

Contents

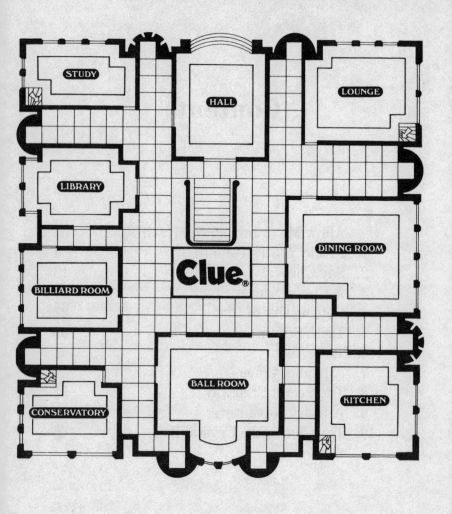

Allow Me to Introduce Myself . . .

MY NAME IS REGINALD BODDY, AND I'M happy to welcome you to my mansion. This weekend is going to be a real scream!

I simply must clear something up right now. Someone has been spreading a nasty rumor that I'm dead. It's just not so!

You remember that on your last visit Mrs. Peacock shot me — at least it appeared that way. Let me explain.

Mrs. Peacock was very angry with me for telling my guests that she learned her manners at a dog obedience school. Of course I told her I said no such thing!

The dear lady didn't believe me at first and tried to shoot me. Luckily, she missed. She soon came to her senses and realized she had falsely accused me.

Well, she was so embarrassed that she began banging her head against the wall. Imagine! The

1

noise was dreadful and sounded just like the revolver being fired — *Bang! Bang! Bang!*

I don't mind telling you that I was so scared I fainted dead away. But I'm not dead.

Thank goodness that's all over! Now we can have fun again. I've invited the same wacky bunch back for the weekend.

Just between the two of us, would you mind keeping an eye on my guests for me while you are here? Oh, not that I think they'll try to murder me again — but just in case. . . .

You have only six suspects to worry about. (I, of course, will never be a suspect!) Let me introduce them:

Mr. Green: It's a good thing that green is his favorite color. When anyone else has any money, he turns green with envy.

Colonel Mustard: He'll challenge you to a duel at the drop of a hat, so don't drop your hat!

Mrs. Peacock: She's a strange bird. Mind your manners or you'll ruffle her feathers.

Professor Plum: Remember his name. He's such a forgetful fellow he'll probably forget what it is, and you'll have to remind him.

Miss Scarlet: Look out for this lovely lady in red. She's beautiful, but dangerous.

Mrs. White: My maid is such a dear friend I consider her a guest. And why not, she's just as deadly as one!

Don't worry — at the end of each mystery I'll

2

give you a chart that will help you keep track of suspects, weapons, and rooms.

Well, let the games begin! Uh-oh. Suddenly the mansion is awfully quiet. That's not a good sign. After all, it's Friday the thirteenth. . . .

1.
Friday the Thirteenth

"**A**H! FRIDAY THE THIRTEENTH! WHAT A lovely day!" Mr. Boddy exclaimed as he strode into the Ballroom early one morning. He stopped short when he saw Mr. Green sleeping in a corner. "Why on earth are you sleeping here?"

"I don't want to go up to my room," said Mr. Green. "It seems that just after midnight, I developed a fear of heights, so I slept down here."

"It's because it's Friday the thirteenth," said a female guest who was sitting on the piano stool. She tapped her red nails on the piano. "We all develop phobias on Friday the thirteenth. Except for you, of course, Mr. Boddy." She let out a sigh. "Mr. Green has a phobia about heights, and I have one about spiders. I've been up all night, terrified that I'll see one."

"I couldn't help overhearing," said a guest who entered the room. "You were talking about phobias." He looked at the other two guests. "She has arachnophobia, and he has acrophobia," he said.

4

"Well, aren't you the know-it-all," said the guest who had arachnophobia.

The guest with acrophobia stuck his tongue out and made a face.

Mr. Boddy frowned. "Oh, dear. I hope the phobias go away soon," he said. "My thirteenth birthday was on a Friday the thirteenth. My aunt, Annie Boddy, gave me this lovely gold medallion." He put the medallion, which had a large number 13 on it, on the mantel. The guests all eyed it and planned to steal it.

"What's your aunt's name?" asked Mr. Green.

"I just told you. Annie Boddy."

Mr. Green frowned. "You just called her anybody? Not a nice way to treat an aunt who gave you such a lavish gift."

Mr. Boddy looked puzzled. Just then a guest with a dirty face walked in and saved him from having to continue the conversation.

"You're looking rather soiled, my good man," said Mr. Boddy.

"I'm afraid I've developed a fear of water and I'm afraid to wash," said the guest.

"Hydrophobia," said the guest who named the other phobias. "Don't be embarrassed. It seems that all of us have developed phobias."

"Thanks, genius," the guest snapped. "What's your phobia?"

The guest scratched his head. "I'm afraid I plum forgot."

"And I'm afraid this is all beginning to bore me," said the female guest. She tapped her red nails on the piano again and gave an exaggerated yawn. "Excuse me, I think I'll go shopping. I saw some lovely red dresses in the window of a shop downtown."

A few moments later the guests in the Ballroom heard a terrible shriek. A female guest waving a feather duster ran in screaming, "Get that cat away from me!"

"She's afraid of the cat. She's got ailurophobia, an irrational fear of common domestic cats," said the guest who knew all about phobias — except for his own.

Another female guest entered the room. "What's the matter with you?" she shouted at the other female guest. "The way you are running around and screaming about that poor little cat is so rude!" she huffed. Then she looked around the room. "Who put the garden snake in my bed?" she asked angrily. "I'm deathly afraid of snakes."

"It's called ophidiophobia," said you-know-who.

Suddenly the last three guests to enter the room noticed the medallion. Like the other three, they planned to steal it.

That afternoon the guests armed themselves with weapons. The one with acrophobia took the Knife. The one with hydrophobia took the Wrench. The one with ophidiophobia took the

Revolver, and the other guests took the remaining three weapons.

After dinner, when all was quiet, a guest crept into the Ballroom and took the medallion. The guest was about to head upstairs when . . .

"Not so fast," said another guest, dangling her weapon in front of her. "What does this remind you of?" she asked. "I'll give you a hint. It's a scaly, slithering thing."

The other guest gasped. She was looking at the weapon that looked most like what she feared. "It looks like a scaly, slithering . . ." She fainted before she could get the word out.

"Ha!" laughed the other guest, snatching the medallion. She wasn't laughing for long, for she heard a noise that made her blood run cold.

"Meow! Meow!"

She fell backward and was knocked unconscious. As she fell, she threw both hands up, which caused the medallion to fly through the air and land at the top of the stairs.

Tough luck for another guest who had been hiding and watching. He was afraid to go up the stairs to get the medallion. He stared at it and paced back and forth in frustration.

It was good luck, however, for the guest who spied the medallion at the top of the stairs. "Yippee! I'm even richer than before!" he whispered.

Plum —
Green - knife
Mustard - Wrench
Peacock - Rev
Scarlet - pipe
White - rope

However, as he picked up the medallion, his luck ran out, because the lights went off.

"Aaaggghh!" screamed the guest with the medallion. "Now I remember what I'm afraid of. It's the dark. I've got nyctophobia!"

Fortunately, however, he had a weapon that could help. Soon he was lighting his way downstairs and into the Study, to study his treasure.

As he walked toward the Study, he hummed a happy tune. He hummed louder and louder, until he sounded like a human buzz saw. Because he was humming so loudly, he didn't hear the guest who was tiptoeing behind him.

Neither one of them was going to get away with stealing the medallion, however, for a third guest was waiting to pounce on them.

In the Study the third guest suddenly leaped from the shadows, shaking a rubber spider. One of the other guests screamed and fainted.

The guest with the rubber spider threw it down and waved his weapon in the face of the guest who was still standing. "You give me that medallion right now!"

"Just let me keep my night-light and you can have it," whined the other guest as he handed it over. "Phooey," he said as he walked to his room.

"Ha!" chuckled the guest with the rubber spider — and the medallion.

Then, he was hit on the head and the medallion was snatched away from him. Just before he passed out he heard a voice behind him say, "Happy Friday the thirteenth!"

WHO STOLE THE MEDALLION?

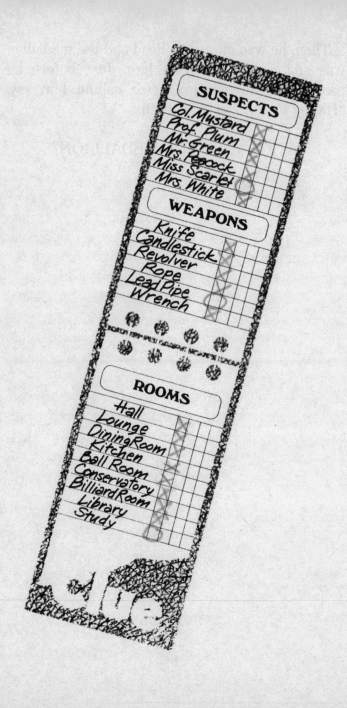

SOLUTION

COLONEL MUSTARD in the STUDY with the WRENCH

By process of elimination we can match all of the characters and their phobias:

Mr. Green, fear of heights (acrophobia)

Miss Scarlet, fear of spiders (arachnophobia)

Professor Plum, fear of the dark (nyctophobia)

Colonel Mustard, fear of water (hydrophobia)

Mrs. White, fear of house cats (ailurophobia)

Mrs. Peacock, fear of snakes (ophidiodophobia)

The only female guest who heard Mrs. Peacock say she was afraid of snakes was Mrs. White. She threatened Mrs. Peacock with her snakelike weapon, the Rope. When she was frightened by a cat, Mrs. White lost the medallion to Professor Plum. Since Mr. Green was the only male guest besides Plum who knew Miss Scarlet was afraid of spiders, we know he was the guest who scared her and then took the medallion away from Plum. That left Colonel Mustard with the Wrench as the one who hit Plum over the head and stole the medallion.

Unfortunately, Colonel Mustard didn't have the medallion for long. He accidentally dropped it into a bucket of water that Mrs. White had left at the bottom of the stairs. He was afraid to retrieve it. The next day, when everybody's phobias wore off, he looked for it, but it was gone. Mr. Boddy had put it in a safe place — his safe.

2.
Say Cheese!

"**E**EK!" MR. BODDY BLURTED OUT AS HE hung up the phone. He looked pale. "Has anyone seen a mouse?"

"Why?" Professor Plum asked eagerly. "I love chocolate mouse. Is there some in the refrigerator?"

"You mean chocolate mousse," said Mrs. White, "and we haven't got any."

"Don't be silly," Professor Plum replied. "How could I eat a chocolate moose? It would be much too big."

"Quiet, please," Mr. Boddy said, putting an end to their discussion. "I'm afraid we have a problem. My sister Minnie just called. It seems that when she was visiting she accidentally left her pet mice here."

"So what?" said Miss Scarlet with a bored look on her face. "Ship the annoying little mice back to Minnie."

"Mice are such rude creatures!" sniffed Mrs. Peacock.

"Tell Minnie I'll challenge her to a duel!" said Colonel Mustard.

"Can we sell them?" Mr. Green asked with a smile.

"What's everybody talking about?" asked Professor Plum.

"Let me explain," said Mr. Boddy. "You see, Minnie forgot to close the door of their cage. I'm afraid mice are running loose all over the mansion."

Colonel Mustard was the first guest to jump on a chair. "Eeek!" he cried. The other guests were too busy jumping on chairs themselves to laugh at him.

"Stop being so silly and get down off those expensive chairs!" said Mr. Boddy. "These mice won't hurt you! They are exquisite, pedigreed white mice. We've got to catch them without harming them, and send them back to Minnie. I know I can count on my dear friends to help."

There were cries of "No way!" "Not on your life!" and "I'm outta here!" The guests jumped off their chairs and began to exit the mansion.

"Stop! Wait!" cried Mr. Boddy. "Minnie must get her mice. I'll offer a prize to the one who traps the most."

The guests stopped dead in their tracks. Then they raced back to Mr. Boddy.

Half an hour later . . .

* * *

14

Half an hour later, the guests were gathered in the Conservatory preparing for the great mouse trap.

Mr. Boddy explained the rules. "You'll each get a cage and a net. We'll meet back here in an hour and see who wins the prize." He sighed. "I know you're all so driven by greed that you'll catch every last mouse."

"How many are there?" asked Colonel Mustard.

"Oh, over a hundred, give or take a few," Mr. Boddy replied.

"We should have some cheese to lure them into the cages," said Professor Plum. "A really strong cheese, like monster."

"It isn't monster, it's muenster," snapped Miss Scarlet. "And I think they'd prefer Swiss."

"It's gouda you to share your opinion," said Mrs. Peacock, "but I happen to know that mice love blue cheese."

"I'm sure they'd rather have a nice mouse-arella," Mrs. White spoke up.

"Stop your cheddaring — I mean, chattering," bellowed Mr. Boddy. "I have a special cheese for the hunt." He opened a lunch pail and took out six squares of cheese. He gave one to each guest.

"All right!" he cried. "On your mouse, I mean, your mark, get set, go!"

Cages in hand and nets flying, the guests scrambled around the mansion looking for the missing mice.

The thought of winning a prize overcame their distaste for the task. Mrs. Peacock was full of enthusiasm as she charged into the Ballroom crying, "Here, mousy mousy mousy."

She quickly captured six mice that were hiding behind a potted palm and grabbed twelve more that she found in the grand piano.

However, when three mice fell from the mirrored globe on the ceiling and landed on her head, she jumped in the air and screamed. The door to her mouse cage flew open and four of her mice escaped.

Mrs. White charged into the room and grabbed the mice that escaped, along with the three mice that had landed on Mrs. Peacock's head.

"Rats!" exclaimed Mrs. Peacock, snapping the cage door closed. "Give me back my mice!"

But Mrs. White was already running toward the Study.

However, she wouldn't find any mice there. Colonel Mustard had already captured all of the mice that were to be found in that room. He had twice as many as Mrs. White, plus two more.

Meanwhile . . .

Meanwhile, Mr. Green was chuckling over his good fortune. In the Billiard Room he had found

16

ten mice nestled in the pockets of the pool table. "I'm having a ball!" he cried, and stopped to make a few practice shots.

"On the contrary, this is your cue to give up," said Miss Scarlet. She seized all of his mice and hurried away.

Professor Plum was extraordinarily lucky. The mice followed him around as if he were the Pied Piper. In no time at all he had two more than the guest with the highest number.

Unfortunately, Professor Plum soon forgot what he was supposed to be doing. He got hungry, too, and sat down and ate all of the cheese left in his mouse cage. As he munched away, two-thirds of his mice escaped.

By now, the crafty Mrs. White had managed to triple her score — even though the mice were deathly afraid of her and ran away from her like crazy. "Come out, come out, wherever you are!" she cried as she ran into the Kitchen. There she found six more mice.

"Gotcha!" she said, as she snapped them up and put them in her cage.

"Not so fast!" exclaimed Mrs. Peacock. She managed to grab a third of Mrs. White's mice before Mrs. White whacked her on the head with a cheeseboard and sent her running for cover.

Mrs. White lost all the rest of her mice, too. Mr. Green stole them while she was hitting Mrs. Peacock.

Time was ticking away and the guests scurried around faster and faster in their quest for mice.

Miss Scarlet tripled her score and then managed to steal one of Mrs. Peacock's mice.

Mrs. Peacock lost all but two of her remaining mice to Colonel Mustard, but then stole all of Professor Plum's mice, plus one of Mr. Green's.

Mr. Green captured eleven more and stole one of Miss Scarlet's.

Then Mrs. White took away half of Miss Scarlet's remaining mice, but lost six of them to Mrs. Peacock.

Three of Colonel Mustard's ran away, and Mr. Green found them.

When Miss Scarlet stopped to powder her nose, she spied six more mice in her mirror and turned and grabbed them. She had just put them in her cage when Mr. Boddy's voice boomed over the loudspeaker, "Time is up! Everyone report back to the Conservatory."

When the guests were all assembled, Mr. Boddy counted everyone's mice and announced the winner. He had brought along his camera to take a photo of the lucky guest. "Say cheese!" he said, and snapped the picture.

WHO WAS THE WINNER? HOW MANY MICE DID EACH GUEST END UP WITH?

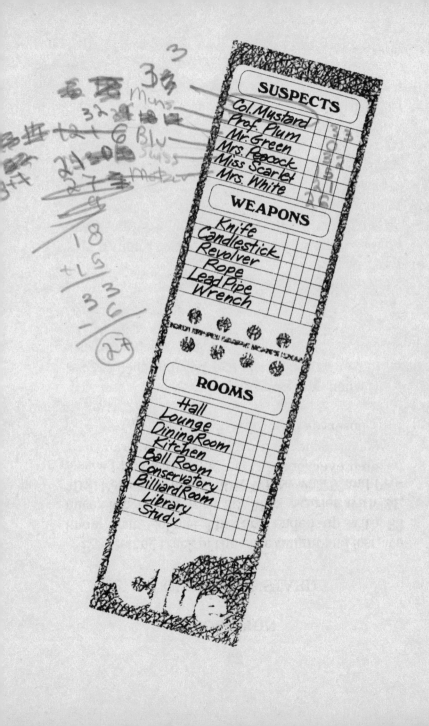

SOLUTION

COLONEL MUSTARD

By keeping track of the mice caught and lost, we know that Colonel Mustard ended up with 33 mice, Mr. Green with 32, Miss Scarlet with 21, Mrs. Peacock with 15, Mrs. White with 9, and Professor Plum with none.

3.
A Flying Saucer Story

MR. BODDY AND HIS GUESTS HAD JUST finished dinner, when Mr. Boddy asked everyone if they believed in flying saucers.

"I know *I* do," said Mrs. White with a scowl. She flung a dish across the room crying, "I'm sick of washing these!"

Mr. Boddy caught the dish, but Mrs. White launched several more. The guests scrambled to catch the dishes before they broke. Finally Mrs. White became tired and stopped throwing the dishes, and everyone sat down again.

Mr. Boddy repeated the question about flying saucers. This time, everyone laughed and said they thought the idea was preposterous.

Then Mr. Boddy astounded the guests with the news that some extraterrestrials were flying in later that night in their flying saucer. They would land right outside the mansion.

Mr. Boddy had arranged to purchase an incredibly valuable treasure from the space creatures — the famous Ersatz Diamond, discovered by astronauts on their voyage to the planet Xaoh.

21

"Is it as big as the Hope Diamond?" one of the guests asked greedily.

"I should hope not," answered Mr. Boddy. "It's *much bigger* and much more valuable. After all, it's from outer space."

Nobody had heard of the Ersatz Diamond, or the planet Xaoh, but they were all eager to get their hands on something valuable. Each guest planned to watch for the flying saucer and be the first to grab the treasure.

"It's a good thing I've taken all your weapons away," said Mr. Boddy. "I'm sure you'll be less tempted to try to steal my treasure."

Little did he know that each guest had managed to take back a weapon and bury it somewhere on the lawn.

Miss Scarlet had buried the Wrench underneath the fig tree.

Colonel Mustard had buried the Revolver near the duck pond.

Mrs. White had buried the Knife underneath the pine tree.

Mr. Green had buried his Rope underneath the swing.

Mrs. Peacock had buried her Lead Pipe beneath the fir tree.

Professor Plum had buried the Candlestick beneath the weeping willow.

The guests all planned to hide on the lawn and be the first to reach the flying saucer when it landed, and get the Ersatz Diamond. All were sure that they had chosen the cleverest hiding place.

That night . . .

That night, Miss Scarlet retrieved the Wrench from where she had buried it, and hid behind the rosebush.

"Quack! Quack! I'm ducking out of here," Colonel Mustard said as he unearthed his weapon and hid by the fountain.

Mrs. White dug up her weapon and hid behind the lawn chair.

Mr. Green retrieved his weapon and hid behind the swing.

Mrs. Peacock carefully pulled her weapon out of the ground and hid behind the weeping willow.

Professor Plum was pleased that he remembered where he had buried his weapon. He dug it up and hid behind the fir tree.

The guests grew restless while waiting for sight of the flying saucer. The guest who had buried her weapon underneath the pine tree decided to hide in the grape arbor.

The guest who was hiding by the fountain moved and hid behind the lawn chair.

The rest of the guests stayed put for a while, watching and waiting. The guest who had buried her weapon beneath the fir tree grew restless. She attacked the guest who was hiding behind the rosebush and knocked her unconscious. Then she returned to her original hiding place.

Soon, the lights of a flying saucer appeared in the sky. The saucer landed, and a bunch of gray creatures with long necks and big heads got out and started jabbering away in a language that sounded like nonsense to the guests.

The guests who were hiding behind the lawn chair, under the grape arbor, and behind the swing, got so scared they ran back inside the mansion.

One of the extraterrestrials was carrying something in a velvet case that rested on a pillow. The two remaining guests figured the case must contain the Ersatz Diamond. Both charged toward the alien who was carrying it, but the one whose weapon had been buried beneath the weeping willow got there first. The guest conked the alien on the head and made off with the diamond.

WHO STOLE THE ERSATZ DIAMOND?

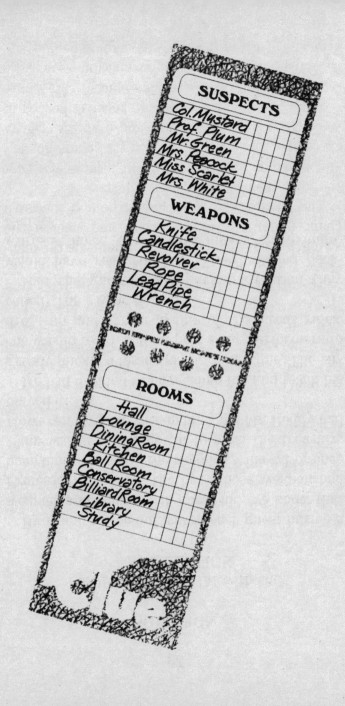

SOLUTION

PROFESSOR PLUM with the CANDLESTICK

By keeping track of where each guest buried a weapon, and where each guest hid, we know that Professor Plum was the one whose weapon had been buried beneath the weeping willow. For once Plum wasn't too forgetful to steal the treasure. However, the joke was on him, and Mr. Boddy had played it.

He had decided to have some fun and teach his greedy guests a lesson at the same time. The circus was in town, and he paid some performers to dress up and arrive in one of the circus rides, called "The Flying Saucer."

Had the guests been paying attention they would have realized that "Xaoh" spelled backwards is "hoax," and "ersatz" means "cheap imitation."

4.
Getting Out of Line

THE GUESTS WERE GATHERED OUT-side the Conservatory. They were waiting to see an extremely valuable show cat that Mr. Boddy had just acquired and was keeping inside.

"Remember that the cat is extremely high-strung," he told them. "You must go in one at a time, or the cat will get too excited."

The guests began arguing about who would go first.

Mr. Boddy had anticipated the squabble and had made them practice lining up the day before. "Quiet, everyone!" he said. "Line up in the order you agreed on yesterday. Cooperate, or I promise none of you will see the cat."

Mrs. Peacock smiled with satisfaction. "Well, at least we all remember where we were standing," she said.

"Yes. The two of you were in the front of the line," said Miss Scarlet sourly, looking at Mr. Green and Mrs. Peacock. The other guests had insisted she stand near the back of the line as punishment for making so many catty remarks.

27

"I had to stand behind you," Mr. Green said, glaring at Mrs. Peacock.

"I had to stand behind both of you," said Professor Plum.

"You still got to stand in front of me," Miss Scarlet told them.

"Well, I had to stand behind you," Mrs. White grumbled as she glared at Miss Scarlet.

"I was last," said a guest who hadn't spoken up yet. "I was quite a good sport about being number six in line." He waved his pocket handkerchief in the air.

"Yes, that is the order we were in," said Mrs. Peacock with satisfaction. "I was number one, at the head of the line. I remember who numbers two, three, four, five, and six were, too."

She was wrong. Neither Mrs. Peacock nor any of the other guests remembered the last-minute changes. They had all been arguing too much.

The guest at the end of the line had made Professor Plum switch places with him. Mrs. White got Miss Scarlet to change places with her by threatening to knock her off her high heels if she didn't. The guest behind Mrs. Peacock stepped in front of her and threw her to the end of the line. She became number six, he became number one, and everyone else's number changed accordingly.

Mrs. Peacock still thought she had been first in line. So did the other guests. It made them very angry. Everyone began arguing all over again.

Mr. Boddy kept his promise and refused to let anyone see the cat. He locked the door to the Conservatory and sent everyone to bed without supper.

The guests all blamed Mrs. Peacock for what had happened. They all planned to kill her.

Later that night . . .

Later that night, the guests all armed themselves with weapons. Number five in line took the Revolver, number four took the Wrench, and number three took the Lead Pipe. Sensing danger in the air, Mrs. Peacock took a weapon for herself. The other two guests each chose one of the two remaining weapons.

The first to try to kill Mrs. Peacock was a man wearing green pajamas. He ran after her as she was walking through the Kitchen, and tried to strangle her by wrapping his weapon around her neck. Mrs. Peacock, however, managed to cut the weapon with a weapon of her own before it did any damage. The other guest was completely shocked and fainted.

"How rude of you!" exclaimed Mrs. Peacock as she picked up the guest's weapon and put it in her pocket. She heard a noise behind her and whirled around just in time to fend off a blow from the Lead Pipe .

"That wasn't polite!" Mrs. Peacock cried as she

disarmed the guest, whom she then shoved into a closet.

"Don't you dare come out of there until you're ready to say you're sorry!" Mrs. Peacock told the stunned guest.

While she was delivering a lecture on manners, guest number five snuck up behind her. Mrs. Peacock saw the guest's shadow just in time.

"Naughty, naughty, naughty!" she said, snatching the weapon away from the guest. "Go up to your room and sit in the corner."

The guest started up the stairs as Mrs. Peacock had ordered but then forgot why he was going to his room when he wasn't ready for bed. Instead he went to the Kitchen for a snack.

The two remaining guests had been hiding since the first guest attacked Mrs. Peacock.

They both decided to rush her at the same time. Right before they ran at her, they exchanged weapons. Then, screeching like Tarzan, they raced into the room, waving their weapons.

Mrs. Peacock saw them running toward her and took off. She sped through the mansion until she reached the room that was farthest from the Kitchen. One of the guests caught up with her there.

"You shouldn't have insisted on being first when we practiced lining up," snarled the guest, backing Mrs. Peacock into a corner.

Moments later the other guest, who was holding the Wrench, entered the room and found Mrs. Peacock lying dead on the floor next to the murder weapon.

WHO KILLED MRS. PEACOCK?

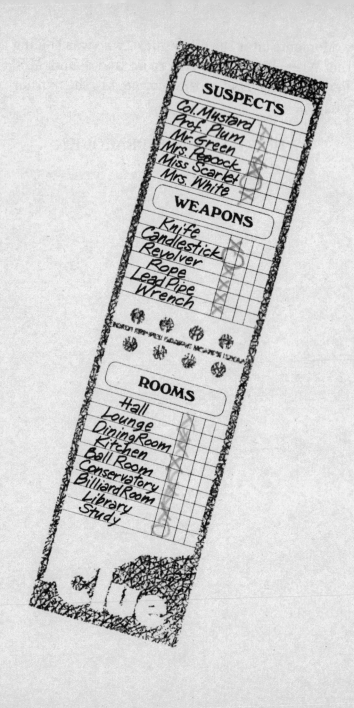

SOLUTION

MISS SCARLET in the STUDY with the CANDLESTICK

By noting the correct order of the guests at the end of the practice line-up, we know that Mr. Green was number one, Colonel Mustard was number two, Mrs. White was number three, Miss Scarlet was number four, Professor Plum was number five, and Mrs. Peacock was number six. The man in green pajamas must have been Mr. Green, who tried to strangle Mrs. Peacock with the Rope. Since she managed to cut the Rope, Mrs. Peacock must have had the Knife. We know that Professor Plum chose the Revolver, Mrs. White chose the Lead Pipe, and Miss Scarlet chose the Wrench. Colonel Mustard had the remaining weapon, the Candlestick, until he switched with Miss Scarlet.

The room farthest from the Kitchen is the Study, which is at the opposite corner of the mansion. While Colonel Mustard was in the Study, Mrs. Peacock revived. She had been exhausted from running so hard and had decided to take a nap. When Miss Scarlet saw Mrs. Peacock snoozing, she threw her weapon down in disgust and went up to her room.

None of the guests ever got to see the cat. Because of all the trouble, Mr. Boddy returned it to its original owner the following day.

5.
Truth Serum

A HUGE CRATE HAD BEEN DELIVERED to the Boddy Mansion and left on the lawn. The guests demanded to know what was inside, but Mr. Boddy refused even to give them a clue. Naturally they were all sure it was a valuable new treasure.

The guests sat around the Study all afternoon and complained about his refusal to give them so much as a hint. Little did they know they'd be dropping some hints of their own soon. They wouldn't have any choice. Professor Plum had mixed a truth serum he had developed into all of the guests' orange juice at breakfast. Professor Plum forgot what he had done and drank the orange juice, too.

Like all of Professor Plum's experimental concoctions, the truth serum didn't work exactly the way it was supposed to. The guests didn't always tell the truth — they just couldn't stop themselves from hinting at it.

"If only we could get our hands on Boddy's new treasure," said a male guest. He looked at the others slyly. "Of course, a weapon would be helpful, and no one has one, right?"

The guests all shook their heads.

"I know if I had one, I'd never leak the news," the male guest continued. "Anyway, without a weapon any hope of getting hold of that treasure is just a pipe dream." The guest frowned and fell silent. He hadn't been able to stop dropping hints about his weapon.

"Well, a weapon would certainly give a person an edge," said a female guest, thinking about her weapon. "It wouldn't be sharp to get stuck without one, no matter how you slice it," she murmured.

"What on earth is wrong with me?" she muttered. "I practically told everyone which weapon I have."

The other guests sensed that something was wrong. "I'm fit to be tied!" a male guest blurted out. "Without a weapon I'm not even going to try for a treasure. I'll just skip the whole idea."

"I don't know what triggered your outburst, but you're absolutely right!" a female guest spoke up quickly. She clapped her hand over her mouth but kept talking. Everyone heard the words, "Shoot! I guess I shouldn't have shot my mouth off."

By now, all of the guests had realized what was going on, although they didn't know why it was happening. The two guests who hadn't spoken yet felt their mouths fly open. They both ran from the

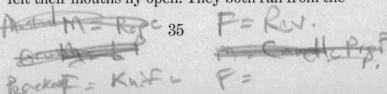

35

room before any words came out. The other guests hurried away, too, before they dropped any more hints.

Later . . .

Later, a guest crept toward the crate. "The idea of getting my hands on this treasure isn't just a pipe dream after all!" he cried gleefully. The guest started to use his weapon to pry open the crate.

The guest uttered one more sentence before falling to the ground. The sentence was, "Wow, that Candlestick hurt!"

The guest with the Candlestick looked at the guest on the ground and scratched his head. "What happened? What am I doing out here on the lawn holding this Candlestick?" he asked himself. He had completely forgotten. The guest took his weapon and went back inside, where he spent the rest of the evening watching television by candlelight.

A few minutes later a female guest with the Knife approached the crate. "I'm the only one with brains enough to steal this treasure," she whispered.

"It's not polite to boast, and you of all people ought to know, since you're supposed to be the expert on manners," said a guest as he tied her up. "Now you're the one who is fit to be tied," he chuckled. He wasn't chuckling for long before he gasped, "I'm shot! I challenge you to a duel!" and fell to the ground.

"What an overactive imagination you have," said the guest who was standing over him holding a weapon. "I didn't even fire this thing."

"And you won't, either," said another guest, who snatched the weapon from her red-nailed hand. "Get lost!"

Then the remaining guest used a weapon that hadn't been used yet to pry open the crate, and cried, "The treasure is mine!"

WHICH GUEST, USING WHICH WEAPON, GOT THE TREASURE?

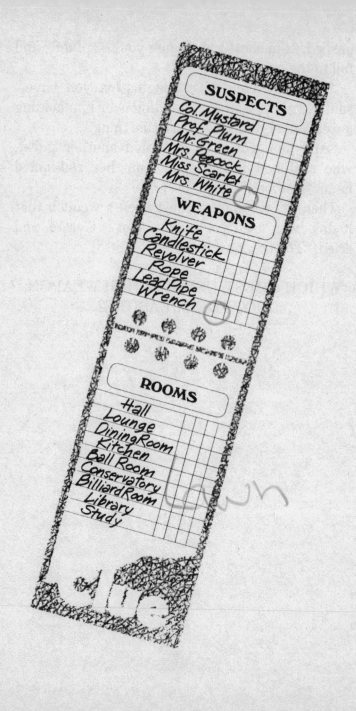

SOLUTION

MRS. WHITE with the WRENCH

From the hints at the beginning of the story, we know that one male guest had the Lead Pipe and another had the Rope. One female guest had the Revolver and another had the Knife.

In the story we learn that mannerly Mrs. Peacock had the Knife, dueling Colonel Mustard had the Rope, forgetful Professor Plum had the Candlestick , and red-nailed Miss Scarlet had the Revolver. By process of elimination we know that the male guest who was struck with the Candlestick was Mr. Green, who had the Lead Pipe. That leaves Mrs. White with the Wrench as the one who got the treasure.

The guests shouldn't have tried so hard. The only thing in the crate was a new bathtub that Mr. Boddy was having installed.

6.
Taste Test

"**H**ERE IS AN INTERESTING ARTICLE," said Mr. Boddy, looking up from his magazine. "It says that most people couldn't tell one soda from another if they didn't see the label on the bottle or can. Taste tests were conducted with people drinking different sodas from plain, unmarked bottles, and a great many couldn't even pick out their favorite."

The guests all laughed. "I'd know mine anywhere," said Mr. Green, pointing to the bright red soda he was drinking. "It's called 'Dentist's Dream,' and it tastes like mouthwash. It's wonderful. I could pick out everyone else's favorite soda, too."

All the guests voiced the same opinion, that they could pick out their own favorite, and everyone else's as well.

Mrs. White's favorite was a pink soda that tasted like floor wax and was called "Spring Cleaning."

Mrs. Peacock's favorite was green, tasted like chicken, and was called "Cluckeroo."

Professor Plum's favorite was orange, tasted like squash, and was called "Squash Surprise."

Miss Scarlet's favorite was purple, tasted like grape jam, and was called "Jammy Jammy."

Colonel Mustard's was yellow and tasted like yams. It was called "Whammy Yammy."

Mr. Boddy decided to have a taste test of his own. He put each soda in an unmarked dark bottle and labeled the back of each bottle so that only he knew which was which.

"Listen, everyone," he said. "I've mixed up the bottles so they are in random order. Each one of you will taste all of the sodas, decide which is which, and write down your answers."

The guests were all sure that the test would be a snap. Mr. Green volunteered to go first. He tasted the first soda. "Hmm, it reminds me of squash." Then he tasted the second. "This has to be 'Whammy Yammy.'" The next he identified as his own "Dentist's Dream," followed by "Spring Cleaning," "Cluckeroo," and "Jammy Jammy." He jotted his choices on a piece of paper and handed it to Mr. Boddy.

The next to test the sodas was Colonel Mustard. "This is that green one," he said after tasting the first. "Ick, it's like grape jam," he said after tasting the second. When he took a sip of the third he smiled. "I'd know my own 'Whammy Yammy' anywhere." The fourth, fifth, and sixth, he identified as "Dentist's Dream," "Spring Cleaning," and "Squash Surprise."

"I'll go next," said Mrs. Peacock. She thought the first soda was "Spring Cleaning" and the second soda was "Spring Cleaning" also. "You've played a dirty trick on us, Mr. Boddy," she said indignantly.

Mr. Boddy insisted that he hadn't, but Mrs. Peacock insisted on sticking with her first two choices. She thought the third soda was "Whammy Yammy," followed by "Jammy Jammy," "Squash Surprise," and "Dentist's Dream." She was angry that her own "Cluckeroo" hadn't been included.

Colonel Mustard and Mr. Green insisted that it was.

"I'll straighten this whole thing out," said Miss Scarlet as she went to take her turn. She quickly went down the line and picked out "the one that tastes like mouthwash," followed by "my grapey one," "Colonel Mustard's favorite," "the orange one," "the one that taste's like floor wax," and "the green one."

Mrs. White was sure that the order was "the purple one" first, followed by "Spring Cleaning," "the red one," "Cluckeroo," "Professor Plum's favorite," and "Whammy Yammy."

Now only Professor Plum was left. "Oh, dear," he said. "I'm afraid I've forgotten what they all taste like."

"Give it a try," urged Mr. Boddy. "Just do your

best. I'm sure you remember more than you think."

Professor Plum agreed to give it a try. "This is my favorite, I think," he said after tasting the first soda. "This second one tastes like floor wax, and the third one must be Colonel Mustard's favorite." After tasting the fourth soda, he thought for a moment and said, "It's Mr. Green's favorite." He identified number five as "that purple one" and number six as "Cluckeroo." Professor Plum hurriedly scribbled down his list of choices on a scrap of paper and handed it to Mr. Boddy.

"You're all in for a surprise," said Mr. Boddy. He poured each soda into a clear glass. They were in this order: orange, pink, yellow, red, purple, green.

WHICH GUEST GOT THEM ALL RIGHT?

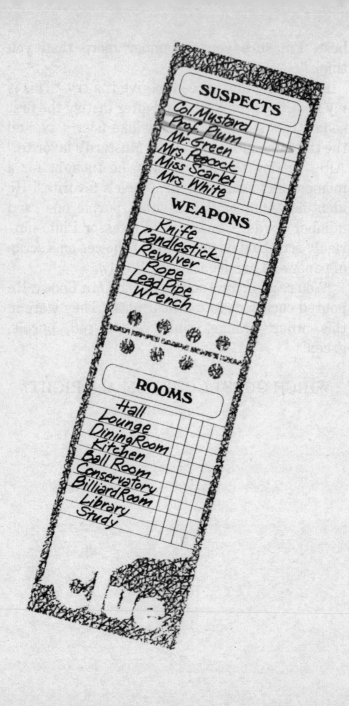

SOLUTION

PROFESSOR PLUM

To find the solution, we only have to keep track of the name, color, and flavor of each soda, as well as everyone's favorite. Although Professor Plum had forgotten most of that information, he made lucky guesses and surprised everyone by naming every soda correctly.

7.
Alphabet Clues

"I THINK IT'S TERRIBLY TACKY," SAID
Miss Scarlet as she looked at Mr. Boddy's latest
purchase — a necklace containing every letter of
the alphabet.

The other guests expressed similar opinions.

"I disagree," said Mr. Boddy. "I think the necklace is, well . . . fun. And the alphabet is made of
diamonds, rubies, and emeralds."

"That *is* fun," said Miss Scarlet. "I love it."

Suddenly everyone else loved it, too. And they
all thought they would love to steal it.

Mr. Boddy put the necklace into a display case
and locked it. Of course, none of his guests ever let
a little thing like a lock stand in their way.

The first to take the necklace was a guest with a
five-letter name. He entered the room with two
words and five more letters than his name, and
used a five-letter weapon to pry open the display
case. He then carried the necklace into a room that
began with the same letter as the weapon he carried.

Unfortunately for him, however, a female guest

46

whose name also had five letters saw him come in and hid behind the door. When he turned around, she attacked him with the only weapon that is two words. She got the necklace away from him and ran into the room with the most letters in a single word.

There, the guest with the shortest name attacked her using the weapon with the most letters. He then hid the necklace in the room that had two more letters than his name. Then he went to his room.

Why did he hide the necklace instead of taking it with him? wondered a guest who saw the whole thing. The guest, whose name was next-to-last in alphabetical order, didn't really care about the reason. She was glad to get her hands on the necklace. She had just grabbed it when she was surprised by another guest whose name had the same number of letters as her own.

"Hand it over, lady!" screamed the other guest, and charged at her, waving a weapon that was last in alphabetical order.

"Not on your life," said the guest who held the necklace. She wrestled the other guest's weapon away, hit her on the head and ran off with the necklace. She saw Mr. Boddy out of the corner of her eye, and hid in a room with one word and eight letters.

Unfortunately she ran right into another guest whose name had the same number of letters as her own, and who had a one-word weapon that had eight letters. He attacked her with the weapon, took the necklace, and left the room.

He spotted Mr. Boddy rounding a corner, and ran into the room that is seventh in alphabetical order. He hadn't been in the room for long when he got the creepiest feeling that someone was watching him.

The guest left the room and went into the only two-word room that hasn't been mentioned yet. From there he went into the room with the fewest letters.

The terrible feeling of being watched got worse and worse. "Someone is stalking me, I just know it," the guest said to himself. He left the room and went into another one that nobody had entered that night.

There, he found out that he was right. Someone had been stalking him. It was a female guest who had taken the necklace earlier and lost it. Now she was determined to reclaim it.

"Aha! At last I've caught you," said the other guest triumphantly.

"You followed me here, to a room with the same number of letters as your name!" gasped the guest who had been stalked.

"Bingo!" cried the other guest, who then attacked him with the remaining weapon and took the necklace.

WHO STOLE THE NECKLACE?

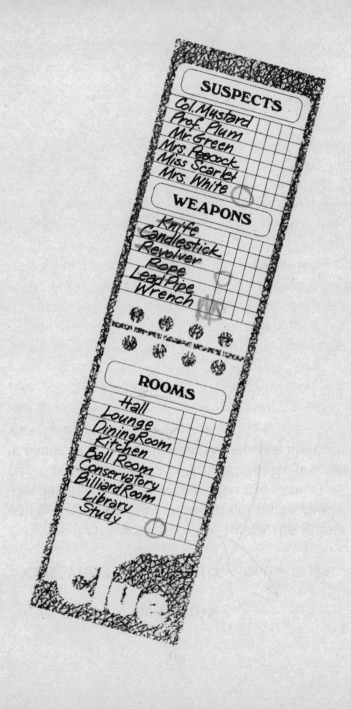

SOLUTION

MRS. WHITE in the STUDY with the ROPE

By keeping track of all the rooms the guests enter, we know that the last room is the Study. The female guest whose name has the same number of letters as Study is Mrs. White. By process of elimination, we know that the weapon she used was the Rope.

8.
The Secret Stairway

*K*NOCK KNOCK KNOCK.

"What on earth is that noise?" Mrs. White asked herself as she leaned against the door and frowned.

Knock knock knock.

Mrs. White turned around and shouted, "Stop making that noise!"

"Open the door!" someone on the other side shouted back. "That's what you do when you hear that noise!"

Mrs. White flung open the door and found a soggy Professor Plum standing outside in the rain. "You're supposed to use the doorbell when you want to come in," she said. "That's why Mr. Boddy had it installed."

Professor Plum drooped in and flung his hands in the air. "Don't be silly," he said. "I've just had a hair-raising escapade. I fell down some stairs and wound up outside."

"That's ridiculous," said Mrs. White. "There are no stairways in the mansion that lead outside."

"That isn't true," said Mr. Boddy as he entered the room. "I had a secret stairway built some years ago when I thought my guests might try to kill me. It would enable me to escape, you see. At the bottom of the stairway is a door that leads to a tunnel that leads to another door. Go through it and you're outside."

By now the rest of the guests had gathered around and were listening with rapt attention. If Mr. Boddy had a secret escape route, they wanted to know about it in case they planned to kill him.

"Where is it?" the guests all asked at once.

"I'm afraid I don't know," said Mr. Boddy. "You see, the fellow who built it was a bit strange. He said that I told him to build a secret stairway, and if he told me where it was, then it wouldn't be a secret anymore." Mr. Boddy's lips twitched in a smile. "Guess what the fellow's name was," Mr. Boddy said.

"Banister!" the guests shouted.

"How did you know?" Mr. Boddy asked, puzzled.

"Lucky guess!" they all answered in unison.

Mrs. Peacock spoke up. "Mr. Boddy, you didn't let Mr. Banister get away with that foolishness, did you? Surely you made him tell you where the secret stairway was."

Mr. Boddy shook his head. "I let Banister slide.

It took him a month to build the stairway, and by then I wasn't scared anymore."

The guests wanted to know where the stairway was. They urged Mr. Boddy to get Mr. Banister to come to the mansion.

When Mr. Banister arrived, however, he refused to tell them where the stairway was, even when Colonel Mustard challenged him to a duel. After much wheedling and coaxing, plus the promise of a huge cash payment, he agreed to give some clues.

"The room had just been redecorated," he said. "I remember you mentioned that you had just finished the week before, Mr. Boddy."

"Why, that isn't much of a clue!" Mr. Boddy cried. "I finished redecorating all of the rooms except the Kitchen and the Dining Room the week before you arrived."

Mr. Banister shrugged. "The room had lots of pictures."

Mr. Boddy stroked his chin. "That could be the Study, the Hall, the Library, the Billiard Room, or the Lounge," he said.

"I remember the year that I built it was the rainiest year ever. It rained day after day after day."

The guests frowned, wondering how on earth that was supposed to help them find the secret staircase.

"I remember that year," said Professor Plum. "I

didn't come to the mansion because I forgot where I put my raincoat."

"Yes, you did come," snapped Mr. Green. "I saw you with my own eyes. The one who stayed away was Miss Scarlet. We all missed the lovely lady."

"Well, I didn't show up that year, either," said Colonel Mustard. "I spent the year dueling for dollars. Did anybody miss me?"

Nobody answered.

"Please continue, Mr. Banister," Mr. Boddy urged.

Mr. Banister started to open his mouth, when Mrs. Peacock began speaking.

"I remember that after you redecorated, I hated the Library, the Lounge, the Conservatory, and the Hall," she said. "I hated the rooms so much that I refused to go into them for an entire year. I like them now, however."

"I felt the same way about the Study, the Billiard Room, and the Ballroom," said Mr. Green. I wouldn't go into them for a year. Funny, I like them now."

"It isn't funny, it's just silly to refuse to go into a room for a year," said Mrs. White, scowling.

"Now, now, Mrs. White," said Mr. Boddy. "You're forgetting that you refused to dust the Hall, the Conservatory, the Billiard Room, and the Ballroom for a year because you hated the way they had been redecorated."

"Thanks for reminding me," snapped Mrs. White. Her face had turned bright red.

"Please go on, Mr. Banister," said Mr. Boddy. "By the way, was the room dusty?"

"I didn't notice," he said, "but I remember it had red rugs."

"That could be the Billiard Room, the Lounge, the Conservatory, or the Ballroom." Mr. Boddy folded his arms. "I'm afraid you're not making this very easy."

Mr. Banister was laughing. He had a strange, cackling laugh. If a chicken could laugh, it would sound like Mr. Banister.

"You put carpeting in your Ballroom? How silly of you!" Mr. Banister stopped cackling long enough to get the words out.

"Well, I had it removed," said Mr. Boddy, looking embarrassed. "Just get on with the clues, please."

Mr. Banister managed to stop laughing. He glanced at his watch. "I only have time for one more clue," he said. "The room contained a huge marble sculpture of a woodchuck."

"But I have one in the Study, the Hall, the Billiard Room, the Conservatory, and the Ballroom," said Mr. Boddy. "That doesn't help me."

Professor Plum paced back and forth. "Drat! I know I found that stairway, but I forget where it was," he muttered.

55

"I've got it! I've got it!" a female guest blurted out. "I know where the secret stairway is. In fact, I just remembered talking to you while you built it."

WHERE WAS THE SECRET STAIRWAY?
WHO GUESSED IT?

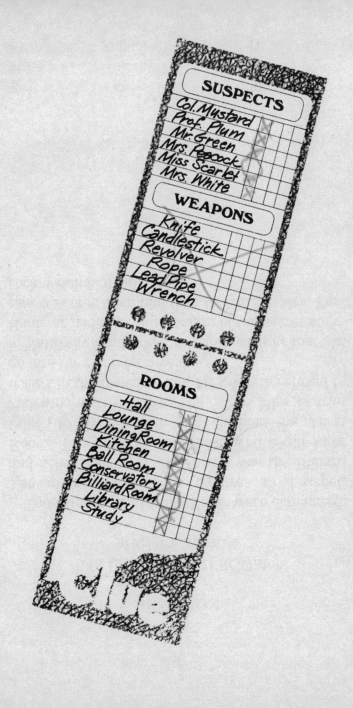

SOLUTION

In the BILLIARD ROOM
MRS. PEACOCK

The Kitchen and Dining Room were eliminated. The only room with lots of pictures, a red carpet, and a sculpture of a woodchuck was the Billiard Room. The only female guest who could have talked to Mr. Banister while he built the secret stairway was Mrs. Peacock, since Miss Scarlet wasn't in the mansion, and Mrs. White refused to go into the room for a year.

Naturally Mr. Boddy was pretty angry that Mr. Banister had kept the location of the secret staircase a secret from him, but he had let Mrs. Peacock watch him build it.

9.
A Hairy Adventure

MR. BODDY RETURNED TO THE MANsion from a trip into town, carrying a shopping bag.

"I have a real treat for everyone," he said. "Something to liven things up around here."

"What are you up to, Mr. Boddy?" asked Mrs. Peacock. "I hope it is nothing too wild or rude."

"Lighten up, Mrs. Peacock," said Mr. Boddy. "I thought we'd try some of the new wild hair colors. I've got bottles of dye right here."

"Hair color? You've really flipped your wig this time," said Mr. Green.

Before anyone could say anything else, Miss Scarlet spoke up.

"Is that stuff permanent?"

"No, no," Mr. Boddy explained. "It isn't a home permanent. It's hair color." He scratched his head. "I'm not sure how long it lasts, but let's not worry about it. Let's throw caution to the wind."

Mr. Boddy emptied the contents of the bag and discovered there were only six bottles of hair color inside — only enough for the guests to use. Then he made another discovery. The labels had fallen off the bottles. He convinced everyone that it would be even more fun to be surprised.

Miss Scarlet hoped her hair would turn a shocking shade of red, which was her favorite color.

The other guests hoped for their favorite colors also. Mrs. Peacock hoped for blue, Colonel Mustard hoped for yellow, Professor Plum for violet, Mr. Green for green, and Mrs. White wanted white.

Miss Scarlet's hair, however, turned pink. She was envious of Mr. Green, whose hair turned her own favorite color.

Mrs. Peacock didn't get her favorite color, either. That color went to Mrs. White, while her own hair turned orange.

"I got what I wanted," said a male guest admiring his locks in a mirror.

"Me, too," said another male guest.

Those two weren't happy for long, because a moment later the colors changed. Then the two male guests were wearing each other's favorite.

Miss Scarlet was happy, though, for her hair turned from pink to deep red, while Mr. Green's lightened to pink.

Mrs. Peacock's hair turned her favorite color. She laughed at Mrs. White, whose hair had changed color, too. "Your hair is that hideously vulgar color that mine was at first. I hate it more than any other."

"Well, I don't," sniffed Mrs. White. "I hate the color Mr. Green's is now."

Everyone gasped in horror as their hair first frizzed, then stuck straight out and changed color again.

Miss Scarlet's was the color Mrs. Peacock's had turned at first.

Mrs. Peacock's was the color of Mr. Green's second change.

Colonel Mustard's was Mr. Green's favorite.

Professor Plum's was the color Mrs. White's had turned at first.

Mrs. White's was the color that Mr. Green's had turned at first.

Mr. Green's was the color that Professor Plum's had turned the second time.

The guests hadn't time to recover from the shock of this third change when their hair changed color a fourth time.

Miss Scarlet's turned the color of Colonel Mustard's second change.

Mrs. Peacock's turned the color of Mrs. White's third change.

Colonel Mustard's was the color Miss Scarlet's turned on the third go-round.

Professor Plum's was the color Miss Scarlet's turned at first.

Mr. Green's was the color Mrs. Peacock hated the most.

Mrs. White's was the color she hated the most.

"Quick!" said Mr. Boddy, dousing everyone with a bucket of water. "Shampoo!" he said as he ran around and squeezed shampoo on everyone's head. They began shampooing vigorously.

WHAT COLOR WAS EVERYONE'S HAIR RIGHT BEFORE THE SHAMPOO?

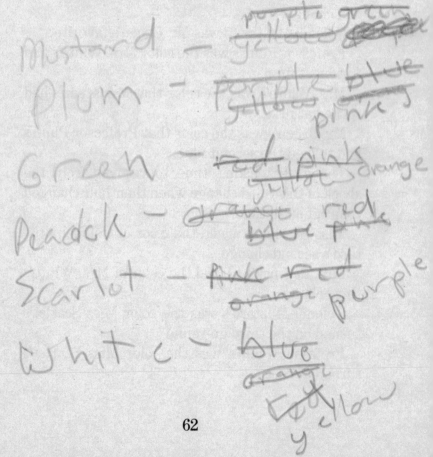

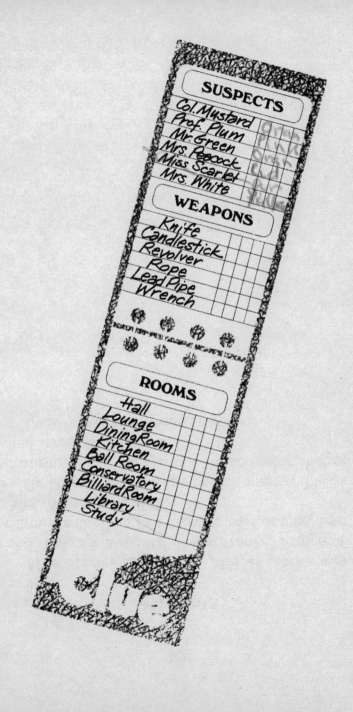

SOLUTION

Miss Scarlet's was violet, Mrs. Peacock's was red, Colonel Mustard's was orange, Professor Plum's was pink, Mr. Green's was orange, and Mrs. White's was pink.

By keeping track of the guests' most and least favorite colors, we can follow each color change and arrive at the solution.

Luckily the color washed right out.

10.
The Clue in the
Crystal Ball

THE GUESTS STOOD IN THE Study, grumbling among themselves. Mr. Boddy had asked them to gather there to view his new goldfish. They didn't think there was anything exciting about looking at a goldfish.

When Mr. Boddy appeared, he explained that he hadn't been talking about a goldfish, but a solid-gold fish.

"Am I herring you right, Mr. Boddy?" asked Mrs. Peacock. "Did you say a solid-gold fish?"

"That's exactly what he said," interrupted Colonel Mustard. "That fish is obviously solid gold. Twenty-four carat, I'd say." He looked pleadingly at Mr. Boddy. "Give it to me," he begged. "My parents never gave me a goldfish as a child. All the other kids had them."

"I'm sure that's not true," said Mr. Boddy. "And it's very shellfish of you to ask for this fish. I'm the sole owner."

The guests demanded to know what Mr. Boddy was going to do with the fish. He explained that he would display it in a bulletproof case that was completely burglarproof.

The guests all laughed at that. They had all broken through Mr. Boddy's foolproof systems at one time or another.

I'll cut that fish right out of the display case, thought Mr. Green as he toyed with the Knife in his pocket.

I'll Wrench that fish away from Boddy, thought Colonel Mustard.

Miss Scarlet touched her necklace, which she had made by braiding a weapon. *Maybe I can lasso that fish*, she thought.

Too bad the case is bulletproof, or my weapon would be just the thing, thought Professor Plum. He was sure he'd find a way to steal the fish.

"I'll bet my weapon can break that glass," whispered Mrs. Peacock to Mrs. White.

"Oh, yeah? Well, I'll bet mine can, too," Mrs. White retorted.

This time, however, Mr. Boddy had the guests stumped. The only way to open the case was to know the secret password. Mr. Boddy wasn't about to tell them what it was. In fact, the guests were behaving so badly he refused to tell even them where the fish would be displayed.

After Mr. Boddy was gone, the guests discussed the situation. They agreed that finding the room that had the display case would be easy, but figuring out the password would be impossible. They were all very discouraged.

Then, at the same time, they all turned to look at the crystal ball that stood in a corner of the Study.

"Let's ask the crystal ball about the password," said Professor Plum.

The others didn't like the idea. They reminded Professor Plum that the genie in the crystal ball didn't like them, and always tricked them and gave them scrambled answers. However, after a few minutes they all agreed they had no choice but to give the crystal ball a try.

The guests all sat around the crystal ball, rubbing it and asking for the password. Finally these letters appeared: ETG TSLO.

"Etg tslo!" Professor Plum cried. "The password is 'etg tslo'!" He got so excited that he jumped to his feet, sending his chair crashing against Mrs. Peacock's. They both dropped their weapons. Mrs. Peacock picked up Professor Plum's. Professor Plum picked up Mrs. Peacock's.

Miss Scarlet examined the letters in the crystal ball. "The answer is scrambled, silly," she said.

This made Professor Plum very unhappy. "I can never, ever, figure those things out," he said.

The other guests quickly unscrambled the letters to form the words GET LOST.

"GET LOST!" said Professor Plum, jumping up and down. "The password is 'get lost'!"

The other guests explained that the genie was just playing another trick and telling them all to get lost. Immediately more letters formed in the crystal ball: OOFLED UYO.

Professor Plum frowned. "Is that the password?" he asked, as the rest of the guests rolled their eyes.

The genie appeared in the crystal ball. "Fooled you!" he cried. "It means that I fooled you and I'll never tell you what the password is. Get lost!" He scowled at them.

Colonel Mustard and Mr. Green jumped to their feet, eyes blazing with fury. They both accidentally dropped their weapons. Colonel Mustard picked up Mr. Green's, and Mr. Green picked up Colonel Mustard's.

"Why you . . . ," Colonel Mustard sputtered, shaking his fist at the genie. "I think I'll smash your crystal ball."

"Uh-uh-uh," cautioned the genie, with a smirk on his face. "Breaking a crystal ball is very bad luck. Very bad."

Colonel Mustard ignored the warning. "That'll fix you for good," he said when the ball lay in smithereens on the floor. The genie vanished, but the sound of his eerie "Ha, ha, ha, you'll be sorry" hung in the air.

Miss Scarlet had been eyeing Mrs. White's

weapon. Thinking that it was more effective than her own, she took advantage of the distraction to switch their weapons.

The guests split up to search for the display case.

Mr. Green went to the Lounge.

Colonel Mustard went to the Billiard Room.

Mrs. Peacock went to the Library.

Mrs. White went to the Dining Room.

Miss Scarlet went to the Conservatory.

Professor Plum went to the Ballroom.

Nobody found the display case.

"Phooey," muttered Miss Scarlet. Letters appeared on the wall before her eyes. OOT ABD.

"Too bad," she read as she unscrambled the words, just as the genie grabbed her weapon and shoved her into a closet.

"Nice NITLCAEDCSK," said the genie with a satisfied smile. He went into the Billiard Room, stole the weapon belonging to the guest he found there, and shoved him into a closet.

Then he raced through the mansion and stole weapons belonging to two more guests, and shoved the guests into closets.

"Now I've added the RCNEWH and the EERRVVLO to my collection of weapons," the genie said.

Meanwhile, the two remaining guests were checking the remaining rooms.

One of the guests was searching for the display

case when Mr. Boddy came into the room. The guest demanded to know the password, but Mr. Boddy refused. The guest killed Mr. Boddy, then ran from the room, through the Hall, and into the Study.

The guest found another guest standing before the display case which held the solid-gold fish. Beside the display case was the crystal ball.

"Hey, I thought this thing was broken," whispered the guest who killed Mr. Boddy.

"Me, too," said the other guest. "I guess it's magic."

Both guests examined the letters that appeared in the crystal ball: DORFISSWH.

"I'll bet it's the password, but I can never, ever, unscramble those things," said one guest sadly.

"Well, I can," said the guest who killed Mr. Boddy, and did just that.

WHO KILLED MR. BODDY?
WHAT WAS THE PASSWORD?

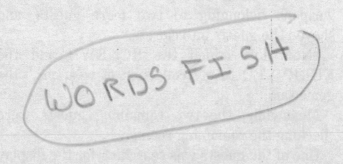

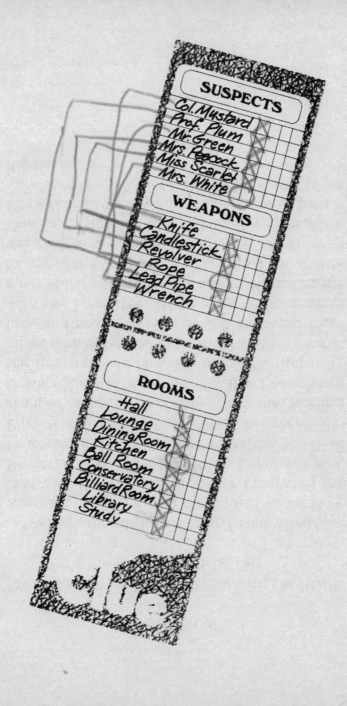

SOLUTION

MRS. WHITE in the KITCHEN with the ROPE
Password: SWORDFISH

We know that the guests started out with these weapons: Mr. Green with the Knife, Colonel Mustard with the Wrench, Professor Plum with the Revolver, Miss Scarlet with the Rope, and Mrs. Peacock and Mrs. White each with either the Lead Pipe or the Candlestick. After the guests exchanged weapons, Mr. Green had the Wrench, Colonel Mustard had the Knife, Mrs. Peacock had the Revolver, and Mrs. White had the Rope. By unscrambling letters we learn that Miss Scarlet had the Candlestick, so that left Professor Plum with the Lead Pipe. By keeping track of which guest searched which room, and unscrambling the letters of the weapons, we know that two guests were left in the Study at the end of the story — Professor Plum and Mrs. White. Since Professor Plum could never, ever unscramble words, it must have been Mrs. White who killed Mr. Boddy in the Kitchen.

Get a clue...
Your favorite board game is a mystery series!

by A.E. Parker

Available wherever you buy books, or use this order form

Scholastic Inc., P.O. Box 7502, 2931 East McCarty Street, Jefferson City, MO 65102

Please send me the books I have checked above. I am enclosing $_____ (please add $2.00 to cover shipping and handling). Send check or money order—no cash or C.O.D.s please.

Name_____**Birthdate**_____

Address_____

City_____**State/Zip**_____

Please allow four to six weeks for delivery. Offer good in U.S. only. Sorry mail orders are not available to residents of Canada. Prices subject to change. CL996